Cherish your memor

Dana Lehman

Remember When...

Written by Dana Lehman

Illustrated by Judy Lehman

Lehman
Publishing
ALLENTON, MICHIGAN

Published by Lehman Publishing
15997 Hough Road
Allenton, Michigan 48002
www.lehmanpublishing.com

Edited by Imogene Zimmermann & Amanda Tackett
Design Layout by Gayle Brohl
Graphic Layout & Design by Dan Waltz

Library of Congress Control Number: 2013919719
ISBN-13: 978-0-9792686-4-9
ISBN-10: 0-9792686-4-8

This story is dedicated to everyone that has lost a loved one.

It was winter break
in Walnut Grove, and
ten inches of fresh snow
blanketed the forest.

As with any break from school,
Sammy's cousins, Silly and Sassy,
were coming to Walnut Grove for a visit.
Many other animals were waiting
for their friends, but
Sammy knew that Silly and Sassy
would not have any difficulty finding him
because Sammy is special. Sammy is a squirrel,
but he has eyes like a raccoon.
Can you find Sammy?

Inspiring everyone to have fun was going to be
a little more challenging this year. One of Sammy's friends,
Bucky (a beaver), had lost his pet frog, Whopper.
Sammy and another of his friends, Rocky (a raccoon)
were determined to make Bucky feel better.
Whopper had disappeared a few months ago.

They couldn't figure out
where Whopper could have gone...

When Silly and Sassy
arrived in Walnut Grove
carrying snowboards,
almost everyone was ecstatic.
Bucky enjoyed snowboarding,
but he wasn't really feeling
up to doing anything.
He missed Whopper.

Sammy said,
"Everyone grab your snowboards
and let's go to Mammoth Mountain."
Sassy could see Bucky was upset, so she said,
"We have looked everywhere for Whopper,
so the best thing for you
to do right now is to stay busy."
Bucky reluctantly agreed.

Mammoth Mountain was enormous.
Silly yelled, "Let's hit the slopes!
This mountain is amazing!"
They all agreed and hopped
on their snowboards.

The day was perfect for snowboarding.
The sun was shining and the snow sparkled like diamonds.
As Bucky was descending the mountain,
his mind drifted to Whopper.
Bucky knew that Whopper would have
enjoyed snowboarding
with him.

Sammy distracted Bucky when he yelled,
"Bucky, look at Silly!"
Silly was snowboarding down a jump and flipped in the air.
They were all captivated.

Snowboarding was one of Silly's favorite sports,
and he had spent a lot of time practicing.
He looked like he was soaring through the air.

Snowboarding was a little more complicated for Sassy.
She hadn't spent as much time practicing as Silly had.
Staying balanced on a snowboard is not easy.

Sassy was amazed with Silly's abilities
and wasn't watching where she was going.
All of a sudden, she hit a rock
and went flying through the air just like Silly…
but not as gracefully.

Sassy landed
right in front
of Rocky,
which caused him
to fall over her.
They both rolled
to the bottom
of the mountain,
creating a big snowball.
Sammy, Silly,
and Bucky
followed them
to the bottom
of the mountain.

Silly asked, "Are you both okay?"
Sassy was the first to respond, "Yeah, I'm okay.
Are you okay, Rocky?" Rocky replied, "Yeah!"
Then they all started laughing.

Bucky said, "I never saw a snowball that big before!
You should have seen your faces!"
Sassy was happy that Bucky was laughing.
At least snowboarding
had taken his mind off of Whopper.
Sassy said, "I think that I have had enough fun
snowboarding for today."

"What else do you have planned, Sammy?"
Sammy said, "How does
ice fishing sound to everyone?"
Rocky enthusiastically replied,
"Ice fishing sounds like fun to me!"
Everyone agreed, and off they went to
Paradise Pond.

Paradise Pond was perfect for ice fishing,
but it was also a place
that reminded Bucky of Whopper.
While they were sitting around the fishing hole,
they started reminiscing about Whopper.

Silly said, "Bucky, you really impressed
me last summer with your swimming abilities.
Remember when you swam out
to that lily pad to retrieve Whopper?"

Bucky sadly replied, "Yeah, I remember.
I really miss Whopper.
Maybe I shouldn't have had a pet.
Then I wouldn't miss him so much."

Sammy sympathetically replied,
"Bucky, if you hadn't had Whopper,
you would have missed out on a lot of good times.
When you think about Whopper and become sad,
try thinking about something that you did together
that made you happy.

Whopper wouldn't want you to be sad all the time.
He loved you and would want you to have a happy life."

"I do have some great memories of Whopper," Bucky replied.
"I guess he would want me to be happy
because I would want the same for him.
Sometimes, feeling happy is hard
because I miss him so much."
Sammy understood how Bucky felt,
but he continued to remind him
of the good times they shared.

Sammy said, "Do you remember how much Whopper
liked swinging through the trees
on our way to Whispering Willows?"
Bucky said, "Yeah, I remember. That was fun!
I think he liked watching us build a tree house, too."

Sammy said, "Whopper will always be with you
because you love him and will never forget him.
You will always have your memories to comfort you.
When you lose someone you love,
healing takes time." Just then, Bucky felt a bite on his line.

He pulled up his fishing pole and was excited to see
that he had caught a big pike.
Bucky said, "I wish Whopper
could see this huge pike.
Where do you think
Whopper could be?"

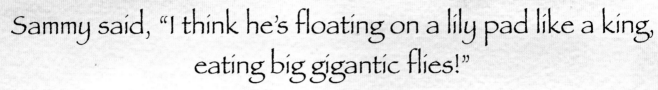

Sammy said, "I think he's floating on a lily pad like a king, eating big gigantic flies!"

Rocky agreed, "Yeah, I think that would be paradise for a frog. Bucky, I'm sure you will see Whopper again one day."

All of a sudden,
    something occurred to Sassy.

She perked up and said,
"Bucky, you might see him sooner than you think.
Don't frogs hibernate for the winter?"

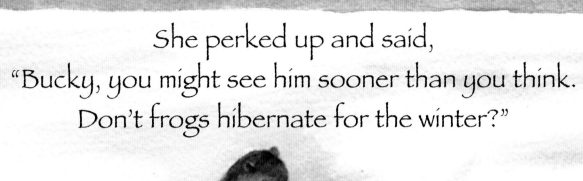

What is your favorite season? Why?

Who was missing in the story?

Why didn't Bucky want to go snowboarding?

Have you ever gone snowboarding?
Do you think snowboarding is easy or difficult?

What should Sassy do to get better at snowboarding?

Have you ever gone ice fishing?
What kind of fish did you catch?

Do you think Whopper would have wanted Bucky
to go snowboarding and ice fishing?

Do you think that Bucky should have avoided having a pet?

Did Bucky have good memories of Whopper?
What were some of his memories of Whopper?

Do you think Bucky will see Whopper again?

A Word from the Author

One of the greatest challenges that anyone has to deal with in life is the loss of a loved one. At times, the loss may seem unbearable. This story was tough to write but very important to me. My father died when I was fifteen. Over twenty-five years later, I still miss him. I wrote about what helped me when I was a child: spending time with my family and friends and staying busy.

Explaining loss to a child is hard because everyone has different beliefs, and I didn't want to bring religion into this story. It may sound crazy, but I wanted to write about this subject without the loss of any characters, and I found a way to accomplish that. This story has a happy ending. Sassy figured out that Whopper was hibernating. Unfortunately, loss rarely has a happy ending.

Bucky had lots of great memories of Whopper. He can be sad, or he can concentrate on being happy for the time they spent together. Bucky was fortunate because he will see Whopper again in the spring. After a long time, I learned that good memories will help me get through the bad days. I am fortunate that my dad gave me many wonderful memories; for that, I am grateful.

Remember When... is Dana and Judy's fourth book in the Walnut Grove Series. They work together to bring these tales of Sammy and his friends to children. All books in this series deal with character education. The first book, 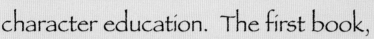 *Adventures at Walnut Grove: A Lesson about Teasing,* teaches children to treat others as they would like to be treated. The second book in this series, *I DOUBLE Dare You!,* deals with a tough subject, peer pressure, and being responsible for your own actions. *Adventures at Walnut Grove* and *I DOUBLE Dare You!* are both recipients of the Mom's Choice Award. *I CAN DO IT,* the third book in this series, helps children realize that with confidence, persistence, and determination, they can achieve their goals.

Dana resides in Allenton, Michigan with her husband and their two children. Her children and love of nature continually inspire her to keep writing children's books.

Dana's mother-in-law, Judy Lehman, is her illustrator. Judy Lehman has been an artist and teacher for over forty years; she is a retired elementary school teacher. She currently resides in Hubbard Lake, Michigan with her husband.